The Pocket Dogs

For D.F., who told me about the pocket dogs—M.W.

For Tanith and Luka—S.M.K.

Text copyright © 2000 by Margaret Wild
Illustrations copyright © 2000 by Stephen Michael King
All rights reserved. Published by Scholastic Press, a division of Scholastic
Inc., *Publishers since 1920*, by arrangement with Omnibus Books, an imprint
of Scholastic Australia. SCHOLASTIC, SCHOLASTIC PRESS and associated logos
are trademarks and/or registered trademarks of Scholastic Inc.

Library of Congress Cataloging-in-Publication Data available
ISBN 0-439-23973-7

10 9 8 7 6 5 4 3 2 1   01 02 03 04 05

Printed in Singapore   46

First American edition, April 2001

The Pocket Dogs

WRITTEN BY
Margaret
WILD

ILLUSTRATED BY
Stephen Michael
KING

SCHOLASTIC PRESS

NEW YORK

Mr. Pockets had a very big coat, and in his very big coat he had two very big pockets.

The two very big pockets were just the right size for two very small dogs. Their names were Biff and Buff.

Every day, winter or summer,
Mr. Pockets put on his big coat.
Then he put Biff in the right pocket,
and Buff in the left pocket.

"Are you ready?" he always asked.

Biff and Buff always said, "Ruff! Ruff!,"
which meant, "Yes, thank you,
Mr. Pockets!"

And off they went to go shopping.

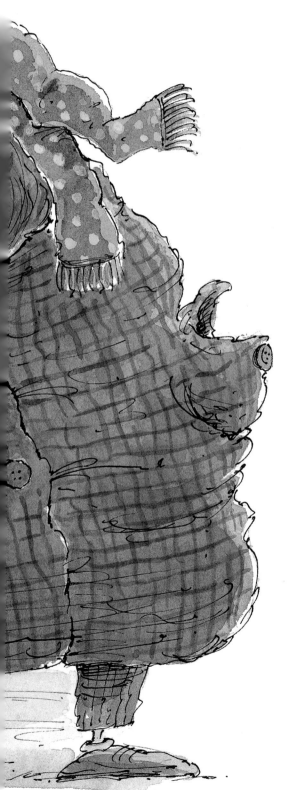

Mr. Pockets and Biff and Buff always took the
long, interesting way to the shops.

Along the way, people always said:
"Hello, Mr. Pockets!"

"What big pockets you have, Mr. Pockets!"

"Hello, little pocket dogs!"

Biff and Buff always said, "Ruff! Ruff!"
which meant, "Hello, people!"

Then one day Biff stuck his foot through a small hole in Mr. Pockets' right pocket.

In no time at all the hole grew bigger

and bigger

and bigger!

Biff tried to tell Mr. Pockets about the hole in his pocket. "Ruff! Ruff!" he said.

Mr. Pockets didn't understand. But Buff did. "One day you will fall out of the pocket," Buff said. "On to the ground. You might get lost!"

"Ruuuuuuuff!" said Biff.

That night Biff had a bad dream.

He dreamed he fell out of the pocket.

He dreamed that he looked and looked
for Mr. Pockets and Buff, but he couldn't
find them anywhere.

Biff woke up, feeling scared and alone.

The next morning, Biff didn't want to ride in
Mr. Pockets' pocket. He hid under the bed,

and in the socks drawer,

and in Mr. Pockets' hat, but
Mr. Pockets always found him.

"What's the matter with you today,
Biff?" asked Mr. Pockets.

Biff tried to tell him. Buff tried to tell him.
"Ruff! Ruff!" they warned. But Mr. Pockets
didn't know what they were saying.

Mr. Pockets put Biff in his right pocket,
and Buff in his left pocket.

"Are you ready?" he asked.

Buff said, "Ruff! Ruff!"
But Biff couldn't say anything.

Off they went to go shopping.

"Hold on tight, Biff!" said Buff.

Biff opened his mouth to say "I'm trying—"
and out of Mr. Pockets' pocket he fell.
On to the ground.

When Biff looked up, he saw legs. Lots and lots of legs. But he couldn't see Mr. Pockets' legs.

"Ruuuuuuff!!" said Biff.

A lady with a shopping basket stopped. She said, "Hello, little dog. Are you lost? I will try to find your home."

The lady put Biff in her basket, and off they went.

But Biff didn't like being
a shopping basket dog.

He was a pocket dog.
Mr. Pockets' pocket dog.

So Biff jumped out of
the basket and ran away.

A small girl who was pushing a doll carriage said, "Look, Mom. There's a little lost dog."

"Let's put him in your carriage," said her mother. "We'll try to find his home."

So they put Biff in the carriage and off they went.

But Biff didn't like being
a doll carriage dog.

He was a pocket dog.
Mr. Pockets' pocket dog.

So Biff jumped out of the
carriage and ran away.

"Hello, hello," said a man with a shopping cart. "I nearly stepped on you! Come with me and I'll try to find your home."

The man put Biff in his shopping cart, and off they went.

But Biff didn't like being
a shopping cart dog.

He was a pocket dog.
Mr. Pockets' pocket dog.

So Biff jumped out of the
cart and ran away.

"Ruuuuuuff!" said Biff.

Biff felt scared and alone. He shut his eyes, tucked his tail between his legs, and put his head on his paws.

"Ruuuuuuuuuuuuuff!" said Biff.

Then Biff felt someone pick him up,
and hold him tight.

"There you are!" said Mr. Pockets. "We've been
looking everywhere for you! Let's go home."

Mr. Pockets tucked Biff into his
big coat, and took him home.

Biff and Buff watched Mr. Pockets
get out a needle and thread and
sew up the very big hole in the
right pocket.

"You were lost, weren't you?" said Buff, and he licked Biff's ear to show he was sorry.

"Yes, I was lost," said Biff. "I wasn't a pocket dog anymore. For a while I was a shopping basket dog, then a doll carriage dog, then a shopping cart dog."

"But then we found you," said Buff.

"That's right," said Biff. "Now I am a pocket dog again. Mr. Pockets' pocket dog."

And he jumped onto Mr. Pockets' lap, and
wriggled into his shirt, against his heart.

"Ruff! Ruff!" said Biff and Buff, which meant
"We love you, Mr. Pockets!"

This time, Mr. Pockets understood.